by **Summer Waters**

Silver Dolphins

STOLEN TREASURES

HarperCollins *Children's Books*

Prologue

On the bottom of the seabed near a cluster of rocks, two dolphins were arguing.

"It's mine."

"No, it's not. I saw it first. It's mine."

They didn't notice Spirit, their leader, a large dolphin with a magnificent yellow blaze along his side, swimming towards them.

"Girls," he clicked, his voice low and calm. "What seems to be the problem?"

Immediately the dolphins fell silent, staring at Spirit in awe.

"I found a shell," whispered Dazzle, the older dolphin. "But my sister Tiny says she found it first, so it's hers."

"Why do you both want the shell?" asked Spirit, curiously.

Dazzle hesitated. "It's pretty," she said, squirming with embarrassment.

"I want it for Mum," butted in Tiny. "She'd love it. Please let me have it."

Spirit shook his silvery head. "Let me show you something," he said.

He swam to the shell that the sisters were arguing over. Gently Spirit nudged it with his nose. The shell rolled over, revealing a tiny mollusc hidden inside.

"Oh!" exclaimed Dazzle. "I didn't realise it belonged to someone else already."

"Me neither!" squeaked Tiny.

Spirit nudged the shell back to where he'd found it.

"It's best not to jump to conclusions," he said. "Always check things first."

Tiny let out a sad sigh. "Mum would have really liked that shell," she clicked.

"Then bring her to see it," clicked Spirit.

"Oh!" squeaked Tiny. "I never thought of that. Come on Dazzle, let's go and get her."

As the dolphins happily swam away, Spirit wished that all his problems were so easily solved. These were bad times for the oceans. If only humans thought more about the consequences of their actions.

Then Spirit remembered the Silver Dolphins. Not all humans were thoughtless. The Silver Dolphins had already made a big difference. They gave him hope.

Chapter One

It was almost the end of another school day. Antonia Lee pushed her long blonde hair back over her shoulder as she put her book in her tray. Then, hovering by the door, she watched the hands on the classroom clock move round to three fifteen.

Hurry up, she thought impatiently, hoping

the teacher would dismiss the class on time.

Miss Brown folded her arms and glared at the noisy children.

"No one is going home until there is silence," she said. "Lauren, that includes you."

Antonia willed the class to be quiet. She had a strong feeling that her dolphin charm was about to call her. Antonia was a Silver Dolphin, a guardian of the sea. Silver Dolphins were specially chosen to care for the oceans and the creatures living there. Antonia wore a magic silver dolphin charm around her neck and it called to her whenever help was needed. Then, using magical dolphin skills, she would swim to the problem and sort it out.

Silver Dolphins were rare. Only people who were in tune with nature and believed in magic

could become one. Antonia knew of two other Silver Dolphins. They were her friend, Cai, and his great-aunt, Claudia, who ran a conservation charity called Sea Watch. Claudia had just recently decided she was too old to do the work of a Silver Dolphin properly.

The class fell silent at last and Miss Brown smiled.

"Well done, 5B. Off you go, then."

Antonia was first out of the classroom, running for her peg, where she stuffed her pencil case into her bag. It was no surprise when her dolphin charm began vibrating. This wasn't the first time she'd sensed it would call before it actually had. Cupping her hand around it so that no one would notice the movement, Antonia called to Cai, "Ready?"

Cai's brown eyes widened in surprise as his own silver dolphin badge, pinned to his polo shirt, vibrated. He lifted his school bag to his chest to hide it.

"Yes," he answered.

"See you tomorrow, Sophie." Antonia waved at her other best friend, who waved a sketch book back. Sophie was mad about art and her latest project was painting pictures of the cats that roamed around Sandy Bay.

"Ooh, look at the lovebirds," called Lauren nastily, as Antonia and Cai ran from the building together.

Antonia ignored the comment, knowing that it was the best way to deal with Lauren.

"Spirit, I hear your call," she murmured as her dolphin charm thrashed its tail and then began to whistle. Spirit was the leader of a dolphin pod and he was responsible for calling the Silver Dolphins.

Cai's badge was whistling too and the combined noise was ear-splitting. Nervously, Antonia glanced up at the parents waiting at the school gates, but only a Silver Dolphin could hear the dolphin's call and no one looked their way as they weaved between them.

"Which beach?" panted Cai.

"Sandy Bay's nearest," said Antonia, her fingers still curled round her dolphin charm. Its tiny tail flicked against her palm, urging her into the sea. She and Cai ran neck and neck down the street, only stopping at the promenade to pull off their shoes and socks. Antonia was first to jump down on to the

beach. Her feet sunk into the soft white sand and it trickled through her toes as she ran to the rocks.

"This'll do," she said, dumping her things against a large boulder before stepping across the rocks to the sea. Cai hobbled slowly behind. It was only the second time he'd answered the dolphin's call and his feet weren't used to walking across slippery rocks encrusted with knobbly barnacles. Antonia hesitated. Normally, she would answer Spirit's call as fast as possible. But she had a strong sense that this time it wasn't urgent and wondered if she should wait for Cai.

"You go on," called Cai.

Antonia was grateful to him for letting her go ahead. What if her feeling was wrong and

14

Spirit's call for help was life or death? Splashing into the water, Antonia concentrated on believing she could swim like a dolphin. The moment the sea reached her waist, she lunged forward. Instantly her legs felt as if they had joined together. Antonia whistled delightedly as she swam out to sea; legs flicking like a tail and arms paddling the water like flippers. She swam clear of the bay and into the open sea before she felt vibrations in the water. Something was coming towards her.

"Spirit?" she whistled.

"Silver Dolphin," he answered. "You came quickly."

Moments later, Spirit appeared and swam straight up to Antonia to rub his nose against hers. Spirit was a magnificent dolphin with a

yellow blaze stretching along his silver flank and dark stripes running from eyes to mouth and chin to flippers. Shyly, Antonia rubbed his nose back.

"What's my task today?" she asked.

Spirit sighed.

"This afternoon a boat anchored up near the cliffs. Two people were diving from it. They seemed to be bringing up things from the seabed. I couldn't see what. When they'd finished they had a clear out and threw their rubbish overboard. It's made a terrible mess."

"Lucky you saw them," said Antonia. Rubbish was a serious problem for sea life and could cause animals to choke or drown.

Cai arrived, panting slightly and with a

determined look on his face. "I made it," he said.

"Silver Dolphin," clicked Spirit, swimming forward to rub Cai's nose with his own. "Thank you for answering my call."

Cai blushed in awe.

"It's litter-picking today," clicked Spirit. "Follow me and I'll show you where."

Spirit set off at a cracking pace, until he noticed Cai lagging behind and slowed down.

"You'll have to teach me how to do the arms," Cai whispered to Antonia. Cai hadn't learned how to use his arms like flippers and was still doing breaststroke with them.

"It's easy once you get the hang of it," Antonia clicked back. Becoming a Silver Dolphin had felt natural for her, but there was

a lot to learn. Antonia also knew there were still things that she hadn't discovered.

Spirit was heading for the cliffs between Sandy Bay and Gull Bay. Antonia gasped when she saw the mess the boat trippers had left behind. It looked like they'd emptied a wheelie bin straight into the sea. There were empty tins, cardboard cartons and an enormous amount of plastic waste; all things that could injure sea life.

"It's disgusting!" Cai exclaimed. "Why do people think it's OK to dump stuff like this?"

"Often it's because they're just lazy," said Antonia.

"And ignorant," clicked Spirit. "Many people don't realise the harm their actions cause."

Spirit had to get back to his pod, so he left

Antonia and Cai hard at work. Cai was lucky enough to find an enormous clear plastic bag that they used to collect the litter in.

"Lucky on two counts," said Antonia. "A dolphin could suffocate in that." She shuddered, thinking of her dolphin friend Bubbles, Spirit's inquisitive son. What if Bubbles had got his head stuck in the bag?

"I wonder what the people were diving for?" asked Cai. "This isn't just picnic waste – look." He held up a soggy sheet of plastic with a label stuck to one side. *"The Stretchy Strap, secures your torch to your arm for hands-free diving.* And there's this," Cai reached out and pulled another plastic bag towards him. *"Dive Bag, made from heavy-duty poly..."* Cai squinted at the label. "I can't read that bit, but it goes on to say that the bag is perfect for bringing diving finds to the surface."

"Weird," Antonia agreed. "It's not like there are any wrecked boats around here. I wonder what they were collecting."

A light breeze came from nowhere, ruffling the sea's surface and sweeping Antonia's hair across her face. She pushed it away, shivering as a bad feeling suddenly came over her.

"What's up?" asked Cai. "You're whiter than a ghost."

"Nothing." Antonia shook the feeling away.

"Oh!" she exclaimed.

"What?" asked Cai.

"Vibrations." Antonia grinned, suddenly feeling much happier. "Someone's swimming this way and I bet I know who."

Chapter Two

A few seconds later, two dolphins arrived.

"Bubbles!" laughed Antonia, as her favourite dolphin surfaced beside her.

"Flipper Feet!" squeaked Bubbles. Then, whipping up the sea with his flippers, he clicked, "Water fight!"

Antonia, Bubbles and Cai splashed water at

each other until Antonia remembered the second dolphin hovering a short distance away. Diving underwater, she swam over to greet her.

"Hello, Dream."

"Hi." Dream hesitated, then gently rubbed Antonia's nose with her own. "Dad said we could play, if you've finished your work."

"We've nearly finished," said Antonia, pointing to the clear sack of rubbish Cai was holding. "We've just got to get rid of that."

"Leave the bag on the rocks for now and come and play Sprat. Race you. Last one there is 'it'."

Bubbles sped off, leaping in and out of the water, his body a flash of silver. Antonia helped Cai with the bag of rubbish and Dream

swam alongside so the three of them reached the rocks together.

"I'll be 'it'," said Antonia once the rubbish was safely out of the water. "I'll give you a three waves' head start."

Everyone scattered as Antonia counted three waves.

"Coming," she called.

The sea was empty. Cai and the dolphins had dived under the water to hide from her. Antonia dived too and was just in time to see Bubbles dart behind a rock. Slowly, she crept towards him but Bubbles had seen her and swam away. Antonia grinned, knowing she'd have to be much faster to catch the little dolphin. Something was moving to her left. Turning quickly, Antonia saw it was Cai. She

chased after him, catching him easily and tagging him as he surfaced.

"Phew," puffed Cai.

It took ages for Cai to tag someone. Finally he caught Dream. Then Bubbles started a water fight by leaping out of the sea, twisting and smacking down on his back. Soon you could hardly see anything for all the splashing. It was Dream who calmed things down.

"Listen," she clicked. "I can hear Dad whistling. It's time for us to go."

"We should go too," said Antonia, "Claudia's expecting us at Sea Watch."

"One more game," Bubbles begged but sensible Dream shook her head. "If we don't go now, Dad might ground us," she clicked.

Bubbles swam towards Antonia as if to rub her nose goodbye, but at the last moment he somersaulted and smacked the surface of the water with his tail, splashing both her and Cai.

"Bubbles," said Dream warningly.

"Spoilsport," clicked Bubbles. "Isn't she?"

Dream looked offended and Antonia held her breath. It had taken ages to make friends with Dream and she felt torn between the two dolphins. Then Cai whispered something, making Dream smile and Antonia relaxed. It was good to see Cai and Dream getting on.

"Bye, Bubbles," she said, rubbing her nose against his. "Bye, Dream. Thanks for coming. It's even more fun when you're here."

Dream flushed. "I enjoyed it too," she said shyly.

Antonia and Cai watched the dolphins swim away, laughing as Bubbles suddenly leapt up and, balancing on his tail on the surface of the sea, turned a full circle.

"The twister," said Antonia wistfully. "I wish I could do it."

"You can do everything else," said Cai.

"Not everything," Antonia protested.

When Bubbles and Dream were out of sight Antonia and Cai collected their bag of rubbish and swam it ashore. As they waded through the breakers on Sandy Bay beach, the water poured from them, leaving their clothes as dry as if they'd been sitting in the sunshine. The only clue that they'd been in the sea was their damp hair. It was a short walk from the beach to Sea Watch, but the rubbish seemed to grow heavier with every step and Antonia was glad when they arrived. They sorted the recyclable things into a separate dustbin before going inside the Sea Watch building, a large wooden shed at the end of Claudia's garden.

Eleanor Jacobs and Karen Holmes, two girls from school, were getting dressed in large plastic aprons and gloves. Next to them was a tall, skinny girl with short curly hair, glasses and freckles on her nose.

"This is Emily Jones," said Eleanor, pointing at the new girl. "She started in Year Six at Sandy Bay Primary today."

"Hi," said Emily, stepping forward and accidentally treading on Antonia's foot. "Whoops, sorry." Emily grinned, showing her metal braces. "We've been asked to clean out

the guillemot cages. It's the first time I've seen guillemots. They're so sweet. I'm going to bring my camera tomorrow and take some photos."

"Hi," said Antonia, wriggling her squashed toes.

"Poor you, having to come to a new school for the last week and a half of term," said Cai sympathetically.

"Why have you?" asked Antonia curiously. "It doesn't seem worth it for one and a half weeks. You'll have to leave again at the end of term to go to secondary school."

"Mum and Dad have bought a shop to sell souvenirs to the tourists, so they're going to be really busy over the summer holidays. We don't know anyone in Sandy Bay. I came to school to make some new friends, so I won't

be bored while Mum and Dad are working."
Emily smiled hopefully at Antonia as if she
wanted to be friends.

"Emily's parents have named the shop after
her," said Karen. "It's called *Emily's Treasure
Chest*."

"Cool," said Cai.

"It's going to be great," Emily enthused.
"Mum and Dad have got all sorts of ideas for
original souvenirs. Mum's going to make them
herself. She's been taking art and craft courses
at night school and she's really good at it."

Antonia gazed round the room and saw
Claudia at her desk. She was on the phone but
waved Antonia over.

"Come on," she said to Cai. "Claudia wants
us."

They walked over, hovering a short distance away until Claudia put the phone down.

"I'm glad you're here," she said, her sea-green eyes crinkling as she smiled. "That was the Sandy Bay Badger Sanctuary. Someone's brought in an injured badger cub but the sanctuary is completely full, so they rang to ask if Sea Watch could nurse it for a few days until they have a free pen. A lady called Jackie is driving the cub over this evening. Could you two prepare the run in the garden we used when we had the seal? There's straw in the garden shed."

"A badger cub," said Antonia, excitedly.

The next hour flew past, as Antonia and Cai prepared for the cub. Antonia desperately wanted to wait for it to arrive, but when she rang home Mum said tea was nearly ready so she wasn't allowed to stay.

"But…" argued Antonia.

"No buts," said Mum firmly.

Disappointed, Antonia set off along the seafront, the quickest route back. The shops stayed open later at this time of year to catch the tourist trade. Antonia wove her way through the crowded pavement until a sign in a shop window caught her eye.

"*Opening tomorrow, Emily's Treasure Chest – original souvenirs that won't leave you broke,*" she read.

Curiously, Antonia stared at the small display in the window. The gifts were certainly original. Who'd think of buying a

toilet-roll holder as a souvenir! It was pretty though. Antonia stepped forward for a better look, then gasped. Was that... no, it couldn't be. She had to be mistaken. Antonia pressed her nose against the window, staring at the shop display in disbelief.

Chapter Three

After tea, Antonia played in the garden with her little sister, Jessica. They made a camp with blankets, pegs, sun loungers and an old washing line. Jessica had just gone indoors to get her dolls when Sophie arrived.

"Hi," said Antonia. "How are the cat pictures coming along?"

"Great," said Sophie. "I found a huge old tabby asleep under a tub of geraniums. The plants made him look like he was wearing a flowery hat. It was so funny. I made loads of sketches. I wanted to start painting the picture tomorrow but now I can't."

"Why?"

"Because we're not going to be here! That's what I came round to tell you. Mum and Dad are pulling me out of school to go on holiday. It's a last-minute thing. Dad realised if we don't go now we won't get one. Once the school holidays start he'll be too busy running art classes for the tourists."

Sophie's dad was an artist and he also taught people how to paint.

"Oh," said Antonia. She smiled wanly and

tried to sound pleased for Sophie, but she was going to miss her friend. "Well, have a good time. Where are you going?"

"Jersey," said Sophie. "Don't look like that! It's only for a week. I'll be back before the end of term and I'll bring you a souvenir."

Antonia shuddered, remembering the souvenirs in *Emily's Treasure Chest*.

"You don't have to buy me anything," she protested. "Just send me a postcard. And I'm pleased for you. Really I am. I hope you have a brilliant time."

"Thanks." Sophie hugged Antonia. "I wish you could come with us. I asked Mum if you could but she didn't think your mum would let you have the time off school."

"She wouldn't," agreed Antonia.

"Sophie!" cried Jessica, staggering across the lawn, her arms full of dolls. "Have you come to play with us?"

"Sorry, Jess, not today. I've got to go and pack," said Sophie hurriedly. "See you soon, Antonia, and remember not to call for me tomorrow."

That night, Antonia lay in bed thinking about *Emily's Treasure Chest*. The more she thought about it, the more uncertain she became. Could she have been mistaken about the souvenirs? Maybe they weren't what she'd thought they were. Antonia tossed in her bed, wishing her racing brain would switch off and let her get some rest. It was gone midnight before she got to sleep and she woke early with her brain still whirring.

"This can't go on," she thought, groggily pulling on her yellow checked school dress.

Determined to find out for sure, Antonia left for school earlier than usual, to go and have another look in the window of *Emily's Treasure Chest*. She hoped that she'd been wrong about the souvenirs on sale. However, standing outside the shop's window, Antonia's hopes were dashed.

Emily's parents had been busy. The window display was finished and the shelves were crammed with souvenirs. There was the toilet-roll holder with starfish ends, light pulls made from seahorses, small dishes made from scallop shells and a strange-looking object fashioned from a sea urchin. A sign hanging from one of the shelves left Antonia

in no doubt as to where the gifts came from:

Our marine souvenirs are handmade from the genuine items.

"It should say, animals have died to make these gifts," said Antonia in disgust. It wasn't right that Emily was allowed to come to Sea Watch, pretending to care. Claudia should ban her.

Antonia hurried to school, anxious to share her news with Cai. She found him in the playground talking to Toby. His brown eyes shone with excitement as Antonia hurried towards him.

"I can't wait for you to see the badger cub," he called as she approached. "Her name's Stripes. She's so cute and not a bit shy. I gave her a bottle of milk last night and when she'd finished, she kept nudging my hand for more."

Antonia had completely forgotten about the badger cub and was pleased to hear some good news. She listened to Cai until he'd run out of things to say, before finally telling him about *Emily's Treasure Chest*.

"It's awful," she finished. "Claudia mustn't let Emily help out at Sea Watch any more. She doesn't care about sea life at all."

"If you're right, then yes, it is awful," said Cai. "But banning Emily from Sea Watch won't help. Far better that she comes along and finds out what we do. Helping at Sea Watch might show Emily that it's wrong to take things from the sea."

"But her parents are killing sea creatures!"

..., her fingers straying to her

...arm.

"...you sure?" Cai persisted. "Lots of shells and things are collected after the animals have died."

"There's too much stuff in the shop for that," Antonia argued.

"Let's see what Aunty Claudia says," said Cai, placidly. "After all, it's not Emily's fault. It's her parent's shop."

Antonia didn't want to fall out with Cai, so she let the matter drop. The thought that Claudia would sort things out tonight made Antonia feel slightly happier. Eleanor and Karen couldn't come to Sea Watch after school and to Antonia's annoyance, Emily asked if she could walk there with her and

Cai. It was impossible to say no. On the way, Emily talked nonstop and asked tons of questions.

"I joined Sea Watch mostly to make friends but also because I love dolphins. Eleanor and Karen have seen them in the bay. Have you?"

Cai grinned at Antonia.

"Occasionally," he said.

"I'd love to see a dolphin. I'm saving up so that one day I can go to Florida and swim with them." Emily chattered on hardly pausing for breath.

Gritting her teeth, Antonia nodded and smiled. *Not long now,* she thought. Antonia was confident that when Claudia found out about Emily's parents' shop she would stop her from coming to Sea Watch.

But Antonia was disappointed. Claudia listened carefully to Antonia's news and then said, "This is exactly the type of person Sea Watch needs. By sharing our work with Emily, we can show her the damage her parents are causing and hopefully she will persuade them to change their ways. Sea Watch isn't just about caring for the sea. It's about educating others to care for it, too."

"But..." Antonia felt awkward about wanting to mention the uneasy feeling she had about Emily.

Antonia was a very powerful Silver Dolphin with extra magical skills because her birthday was on midsummer's day. She had something that Claudia called a sixth sense. It meant knowing certain things without being told them, and Claudia had it too. Antonia was conscious that her sixth sense was getting stronger. She was convinced it was telling her that there was something bad about the girl.

You're wrong about Emily.

Antonia jumped as she heard Claudia's voice inside her head.

Trust me.

Claudia stared deeply into Antonia's eyes until Antonia felt slightly giddy.

I do trust you, she thought.

Then you must give Emily a chance. Promise me?

Antonia tried to look away but Claudia's gaze held her. Then suddenly she smiled so warmly that Antonia would have promised her anything.

OK. I promise, I'll give Emily a chance.

Well done, Silver Dolphin.

Claudia winked at Antonia then steering her towards the door, she spoke aloud, "Come and see the badger cub, she's gorgeous."

Chapter Four

There was no shortage of volunteers wanting to help with Stripes. Everyone had heard about the badger cub and they followed Claudia outside to see her. Claudia insisted that the cub was handled as little as possible.

"Stripes isn't a pet," she explained. "When she's better, she'll be returned to the wild.

She's more likely to get hurt again if she becomes too confident around people."

To Antonia's delight, Claudia chose her to see to Stripes while Cai and Emily were asked to clean out the guillemots. Antonia felt a slight pang of jealousy that she hadn't been paired with Cai, but quickly realised she was being mean. She waved at Cai and Emily as they disappeared indoors to start work.

"The badger sanctuary sent lots of things for Stripes," said Claudia. "Come with me and I'll show you where everything is."

Antonia followed Claudia back inside the Sea Watch building to the small kitchen area.

"That's her bottle sterilising." Claudia pointed at a dainty bottle sitting in a jug of clear liquid on the worktop. "It doesn't need rinsing. Just give it a shake dry, then pour the milk in up to the line. Warm it in the microwave, then shake the bottle again to make sure there aren't any hot spots."

"Where's the milk? In the fridge?" Antonia asked, pointing over to it.

"Yes." Claudia pulled the door open. "It's the blue bottle."

"This isn't cow's milk," said Antonia, reading the label.

"It's a specially prepared milk formula. Cow's milk can give cubs the runs."

"Yuk!" Antonia grimaced and Claudia laughed.

"Sit Stripes on that towel when you feed her to keep your school dress clean. And be gentle with her. She's got a nasty wound on her back leg where she was hit by a car. The bandage shouldn't need changing yet, but give me a shout if it looks like it's leaking. I'll be at the computer," said Claudia.

After snapping on a pair of rubber gloves, Antonia collected a bucket to put the soiled straw in and headed out to the pen. Stripes was very inquisitive, snuffling round her feet as she picked up the dirty bedding. Antonia went back to the shed for clean straw and when she returned, she noticed Emily outside. She was hovering a short distance away from the badger pen. She watched as Antonia put down clean straw and refilled Stripes's water bowl. Then she followed Antonia when she went indoors to prepare Stripes's milk.

"Haven't you got anything to do?" asked

Antonia, irritated at being watched.

"I'm helping Cai," said Emily vaguely, fidgeting with her rubber gloves.

Antonia lifted the bottle out of the sterilising fluid, waved it dry and filled it up to the line with the special milk. It took seconds to warm in the microwave. After screwing the teat on the top, she shook the bottle, picked up the towel and went to feed Stripes. The badger cub nudged at the bottle teat with her black button nose. Laughing, Antonia lifted her on to her lap, then guided the teat into Stripes's mouth.

"Hungry, are we?" she held the bottle tightly as Stripes began to suck.

The baby badger looked so cute, Antonia wanted to stroke her black and white face but,

remembering Claudia's warning, she didn't. Emily edged closer, then hesitantly stepped inside the pen.

"How old is she?"

"About ten weeks."

"She's gorgeous," breathed Emily.

Antonia's hair swung away from her face as she smiled up at Emily.

"Isn't she just!"

"Oh! Look at your necklace," Emily reached forward.

Scowling, Antonia pulled back shaking her head so her hair covered her dolphin charm.

"Sorry, I didn't mean to upset you. That necklace is beautiful too. Was it very expensive?"

"It was a gift," said Antonia.

Emily sighed. "I don't suppose I could afford one. My parents have spent most of their money setting up the shop."

Antonia suddenly felt hot and her hands trembled slightly. She had wanted to say something to Emily about her parents' gift shop and here was her chance. But before she could speak, another sensation swept over her. Spirit! He was going to call and this time it was urgent. Stripes was only halfway through her bottle. Antonia wiped a drop of milk from the cub's nose then, noticing Emily's rapt expression, decided to ask her for help.

"Emily," she said. "I've just remembered I have a really important job to do. Can you finish feeding Stripes for me?"

"Me? Yeah, I'd love to." Emily looked as if

she'd just been handed a million pounds.

"Come and sit down then."

When Emily was comfortable, Antonia handed Stripes over. All the time the cub didn't stop sucking on the bottle.

"Oh," squeaked Emily softly. "Thanks, Antonia."

At that moment, Antonia's silver dolphin charm juddered.

"Don't forget to check the pen's locked when you've finished," Antonia called. "The padlock's a bit stiff."

She hurried down the garden and through the gate to the beach. Leaving her sandals under the Sea Watch boat, Antonia ran into the sea. Her dolphin charm was vibrating strongly and suddenly it gave a shrill whistle.

"Spirit, I hear your call," clicked Antonia, as she splashed into the water.

There was no question of waiting for Cai today. Spirit's call was urgent. The dolphin charm thrashed against her skin, urging her on. The moment Antonia's legs melded together she started swimming, effortlessly flying in and out of the sea, causing a spray of water that sparkled like diamonds. Antonia followed the coastline heading west. She swam fast, anxious to find Spirit.

After a very long time Antonia slowed, sensing two different types of vibration in the water. Looking up, she saw a boat in the distance. That could be causing the bigger vibration. The smaller one she hoped was being made by Spirit. The boat, a small blue

fishing vessel with an ancient-looking cabin, came closer. Nets, hung with fluorescent pink buoys, were draped over one side. A tall lady was moving around on deck. She looked vaguely familiar. Diving under the water so as not to be seen, Antonia tried to work out how she might know her. She kept underwater, swimming on a parallel path with the boat to avoid a collision. The vibrations became stronger and the sea more choppy as finally, the boat passed her by.

"Silver Dolphin?"

"Yes," clicked Antonia, answering Spirit's sudden urgent whistle.

"Get the name of the boat."

Immediately Antonia somersaulted and surfaced so she was facing the boat's stern as it sped away from her. The boat was travelling fast and the boat's name was already too small for her to read. She screwed up her eyes trying to make out its registration number painted in much larger characters.

"SB... is that a 6 or an 8?"

It was no good. Antonia couldn't read the registration number either.

"Did you get its name?" Spirit surfaced alongside her.

Antonia shook her head. "Sorry, it was going too fast. The first two letters were SB so it's a Sandy Bay boat, if that's any help?"

Spirit looked disappointed.

"You'll need more than that to report it."

"Who am I reporting it to and why?" asked Antonia, puzzled.

"I'll show you when the second Silver Dolphin arrives," said Spirit.

Suddenly Antonia was aware of vibrations in the water, pinging against her skin like tiny stones.

"Cai," she remembered guiltily.

Chapter Five

ai swam up. "I came as fast as I could," he puffed.

"Thank you, Silver Dolphin." Spirit swam forward and greeted Cai by rubbing noses. "And thank you, too," he added, ruffling Antonia's hair with a flipper.

"But I failed," said Antonia miserably.

"You answered the call and that's what

matters," Spirit answered her.

"What happened?" asked Cai.

"The boat that dumped the rubbish came back. This time it put down nets in a protected area. It's damaged a bed of pink sea fan coral. Come with me and I'll show you," said Spirit.

He dived down, followed by Antonia and Cai. At first the water was murky but gradually it cleared enough for Antonia to see that they were swimming over rocks. Spirit swum deeper and then stopped.

"We're here," he said.

"It's beautiful," said Antonia, venturing forward to stare at the miniature forest stretching away from her.

"The coral looks exactly like fan-shaped

trees!" exclaimed Cai.

"Each pink sea fan coral is made from thousands of tiny organisms, so they're actually animals not plants. Look again and you'll see the damage the net caused."

"Oh!" cried Antonia. "Some of them are broken."

She swam closer, pointing in dismay at the pieces of coral scattered like broken china around the stems of the pink sea fans.

"Pink sea fans are very fragile," Spirit continued. "They also take ages to grow. This area is protected, but not everyone is aware of that. If you give the boat's details to the coastguards, they will make sure the owners know that the coral reef is a protected area."

Antonia started to swim round the pink sea

fans. It was like swimming in a huge garden of flowers. The corals were so colourful. She loved them all, from the palest pink to the vibrant cerise ones. As she swam, a plan of how to find the boat causing the damage was forming in her head. She was almost ready to share it when she noticed Cai signalling upwards. Antonia followed him and broke through the sea's surface at the same time as Spirit, creating a sparkling blue fountain of water.

Cai gulped at the air with huge greedy breaths.

"Sorry," he panted. "I can't stay underwater as long as you."

"You will with practice," said Antonia.

"Remember you are very powerful," Spirit

warned Antonia. "Not every Silver Dolphin will develop all of your skills."

Cai stared at Antonia in surprise.

"You never told me that," he said admiringly.

Antonia shrugged, letting her wet hair flop forward to hide her face.

"It's nothing really. Listen, I've had an idea. Let's go home and walk round to the harbour. I might recognise the boat, and the lady on board, if I saw them again. Then we can get the name and registration number, and tell the coastguard."

"Careful, Silver Dolphin," warned Spirit. "Some of the boats are very similar. You must be sure you have the right one before you report it. I think you should wait."

"But the owners might come back and cause more damage," said Antonia.

"Spirit's right," said Cai reasonably. "It won't solve anything if we get the wrong boat."

"I suppose not. I just hate waiting." Antonia sighed heavily.

The sea began to churn and Bubbles suddenly appeared from underwater, followed by Dream.

"I never felt you coming," squeaked Antonia.

"Too busy talking," teased Bubbles. "Have the Silver Dolphins finished, Dad? Can they play?"

"They can," Spirit agreed. "Have fun, everyone." Spirit gently rubbed Antonia's nose, saying, "Don't worry, Silver Dolphin. You did your best."

"I can't help worrying," said Antonia quietly as Spirit swam away.

"Seaweed tag," said Bubbles happily.

He dived underwater, then surfacing behind Dream, flipped a crinkly strand of brown seaweed at her. "You're 'it'."

Antonia tried to forget about the boat as Dream chased after Bubbles, tagging his tail with the seaweed before he could dive for cover. Bubbles flicked the seaweed on to his flipper then took off after Antonia, who neatly somersaulted out of his way. Bubbles slowed and rolled on his back as if he was thinking. Then suddenly he righted himself and leapt after a surprised Cai.

"It," clicked Bubbles tossing the seaweed. It fell a metre short and Cai laughed, then dived

under water. Snatching up the seaweed, Bubbles gave chase, tagging Cai as he did a clumsy somersault turn.

"Aw!" Cai exclaimed.

He swam towards Dream then suddenly changed direction and threw the seaweed back at Bubbles.

"It," he whistled, triumphantly.

"Not bad!" clicked Bubbles. "Your swimming's improving. But you'd go faster if you used your hands like flippers instead of that funny thing you keep doing with them."

"That's breaststroke," said Antonia, swimming over.

"Teach me how to do flipper hands," Cai challenged Bubbles.

"It's easy. Just move like this," said Bubbles, demonstrating with his flippers.

Cai copied Bubbles and ended up swimming in a circle.

"It helps if you keep your fingers together," said Antonia.

"That's better." Dream swam alongside, clicking encouragement.

Cai practised some more and managed to swim in a short wonky line.

"Well done," said Dream kindly, as he stopped for a rest.

"That was brilliant," Antonia agreed. "Look how far we've swum. Perhaps we'd better go back now? I didn't have time to tell Claudia that I'd left Stripes with Emily."

"Emily will be fine," said Cai. "She's

really keen to help."

Antonia didn't answer. What if Claudia and Cai were wrong about the new girl?

"We ought to go home," said Dream. "Mum told us not to stay out too long. The pod's going fishing later."

"One more game of tag," said Bubbles. "I'll be 'it'. You get a three waves' start."

Everyone scattered in opposite directions. Bubbles waited for three waves, then sped after Antonia. He almost tagged her straightaway but she darted behind Dream. Bubbles clicked a laugh, too surprised to tag his sister instead. At last, Bubbles caught Antonia, throwing the seaweed so it landed over her shoulder like wrinkly brown scarf.

"Game over," Antonia panted. "Well

done," she added, high-fiving Bubbles on the fin.

Bubbles and Dream swam with Antonia and Cai until they could see Claudia's beach. They rubbed noses with everyone then swam back out to sea, their silver bodies flashing in the sunlight. Antonia and Cai headed ashore at a slower pace.

"I wonder who owns that fishing boat," Antonia mused.

"Fishermen?" suggested Cai.

Antonia shook her head.

"The local fishermen look after the sea. There would be nothing left for them to fish for otherwise. It's more likely to be holiday-makers. They sometimes hire out old fishing boats to go diving from. Or..." she slid a

sidelong glance at Cai. "It might be Emily's parents!" Her voice rose in excitement. "What if they've been taking things from the sea to sell in their horrible shop?"

Cai laughed so much he swallowed a mouthful of sea and choked.

"Wicked imagination!" he spluttered. "Emily's parents are too busy making souvenirs and selling them to go out collecting stuff as well. They'll buy the shells in."

Antonia fell quiet, miffed at Cai for laughing at her.

"I suppose we could go and have a look around the harbour," said Cai eventually. "If you think you see the boat then you could make a note of its name, but not report it yet."

"OK," said Antonia, slightly appeased. "Have we got time to go now?"

"I guess so," said Cai. "We haven't been gone that long. Time seems to slow down when we're with the dolphins."

"It does," agreed Antonia. "I never really noticed that till now. We always get loads done when we're with them."

When the sea was shallow enough, Antonia and Cai waded ashore. Water poured from them and their clothes dried almost instantly. They rescued their shoes from under the Sea Watch boat and sat on the warm sand to put them on.

"We'd better go and tell Claudia where we're going," said Antonia.

As they walked towards the Sea Watch

building, Antonia suddenly clapped a hand over her mouth.

"No!" she gasped.

"What?" said Cai.

His eyes followed the direction she was looking in.

"Emily!" groaned Antonia. "She's not locked the badger pen properly."

The door stood open with the padlock swinging from the bolt. Antonia ran over but she was too late. The pen was empty. Emily came out of the Sea Watch building, carrying an old football. She waved at Antonia and Cai.

"I went to get Stripes something to play with and look what I found," she called triumphantly.

What was Emily thinking? Stripes wasn't a

puppy. Suddenly Antonia was angry with herself for trusting the new girl. Emily reached the badger pen and her mouth opened in horror.

"Oh no!" she gasped.

Chapter Six

Realising anger wasn't going to help anyone, Antonia pulled herself together.

"Stripes can't have gone far," she said calmly. "Emily, you look over there. Cai, take the top of the garden and I'll look behind these bushes."

Antonia crawled on her hands and knees to search. Some of the bushes were so thick she didn't think Stripes would manage to squeeze under them but she checked anyway, lying flat on her stomach for a better look. All sorts of worrying situations flashed through her mind, like Stripes escaping on to the road or falling into the sea. Antonia was beginning to work herself into a state when Emily shouted, "I've found her."

Antonia raced up the garden, reaching Emily at the same time as Cai.

"She's under there."

Emily pointed at a blue flowering shrub from which Stripes's stumpy tail was visible.

"Thank goodness."

Relief flooded through Antonia as she reached for the cub. At first Stripes didn't want to come out and Antonia found herself

engaged in a gentle tug of war.

"Look at her nose," she giggled with relief, as finally she pulled the badger cub out.

Stripes's nose was covered in dirt. Cai laughed but Emily's face crumpled and she burst into tears.

"What's wrong?" said Cai.

"I don't want to leave Sea Watch," sobbed Emily, tears rolling down her cheeks. "I really like helping here."

"Why are you leaving? You've only just started."

"When Claudia hears about Stripes she'll throw me out."

"Aunty Claudia wouldn't do that," said Cai, astonished.

"She's not like that," added Antonia

forcefully. "She never tells anyone off for genuinely making a mistake."

"Are you sure?" sniffed Emily.

"Very," said Antonia firmly. "Anyway, it was my fault too. I should have made sure you knew how to lock the padlock. Come and help me put Stripes back and I'll show you how it's done."

"Thanks, Antonia." Emily looked so grateful that Antonia felt guilty about not liking her. But how could she be friends with Emily when her parents owned such a horrible shop? Antonia forced herself to be extra nice as she showed Emily how to fasten the padlock and let her practise locking it. As they headed back to the Sea Watch shed Claudia came out to meet them.

"Good news," she said, running a hand through her wavy hair. "Jackie from the badger sanctuary just rang. They're definitely releasing two badgers back into the wild on Sunday, so there'll be room for Stripes."

Emily's face fell.

"Does she have to go back? She's only just got here. Can't we keep her until she's ready to go back into the wild too?"

Claudia shook her head.

"This was only temporary. It's better for Stripes to return to the sanctuary. Badgers are very sociable animals and need the company of other badgers."

Claudia reached forward and gave the padlock on the pen door a hard tug.

"Just checking," she said. "It's a bit stiff –

doesn't always lock properly."

Emily blushed but Claudia didn't seem to notice.

"That's it, then. All done for today. Thanks for your help, everyone. I'm going up to the house to make dinner. Are you staying for tea tonight, Antonia?"

Antonia shook her head.

"I can't, thanks. I've got swimming club."

"It's squad-only tonight." Emily rounded on Antonia in surprise. "Are you on the team?"

"Yes. I've just been given a place."

"Wow! You must be an excellent swimmer. They don't usually take you until you're in Year Six. I've transferred from my old club. Tonight's my first time but I already know some of the team from doing competitions."

Antonia stared at Emily in disbelief. Was there no escape from her?

"I didn't know you swam," she said lamely.

"Oh yes," Emily nodded her head vigorously. "I've won a few medals. Dad said I can learn to scuba dive next year. Then I can go out with him and Mum. They love the water. We all do. See you tonight, then."

Emily waved as she loped up the garden in her awkward gangly stride, chattering to Claudia.

"There's not going to be enough time to go to the harbour after all," Cai said. "We used it up looking for Stripes."

Antonia sighed in frustration. "'We'll have to go tomorrow, straight after school."

"Good idea. See you then," said Cai.

Antonia rushed home, ate an early tea, helped Mum clear up the dishes, then went to her room to pack her bag ready for swimming. Jessica followed and sat on the bed watching her.

"I want to be in the squad too. Do you think I'll be good enough soon?"

"If you practise," said Antonia, rummaging in the drawer for her swimming goggles. She found them inside her swimming hat and put both in her bag with her towel, swimming costume, shampoo and hairbrush, then zipped it up.

"Will you play with me now?" asked Jessica.

"I'm going swimming," said Antonia.

"That's not for another half an hour. Please, Antonia. Come and see my dolls. I've made a camp for them in my bedroom."

"Just a quick look," said Antonia reluctantly, but luckily she was saved by Dad, who wanted to leave earlier than usual so he could drop off a quote to a customer.

"This customer's just bought an old fishing boat to go diving from," said Dad as he drove the car off the main road and into a lane. "It needs quite a bit of work on the engine."

Antonia's pulse raced.

"A fishing boat?" she asked. Could this be the boat that was causing the damage out at sea? "What's it called?"

"I've no idea. You'll see it in a minute."

Rounding a corner, the lane opened out into a yard with outbuildings on the long side and a house in the corner. Antonia's heart sank when she spotted an old fishing boat parked on a trailer. It was nothing like the boat she was after. By the look of it, this boat wasn't even seaworthy.

"Wait here," said Dad, parking the car and reaching for a long white envelope on the dashboard. "I won't be a sec."

Absentmindedly, Antonia twiddled her dolphin charm as she watched Dad knock on the front door. As much as she loved swimming, she wished she didn't have to go tonight. Then she could have gone to the harbour before tea with Cai and they might have been closer to solving the mystery of the boat owners, before they caused any more damage.

"Spirit, I will sort this out," Antonia vowed, lightly running her finger along her dolphin's soft back.

The charm juddered slightly and Antonia sat bolt upright. Was Spirit about to call? She concentrated on the dolphin but it was still now and her sixth sense told her she wasn't needed.

"Back again," said Dad, sliding into the car. "Swimming club next."

"Cool," said Antonia, forcing a smile.

The swimming pool was busy and Dad had to park at the end of the road. As they drove past the entrance, Antonia saw Emily walking in with a lady who was obviously her mother.

She was tall and thin just like Emily and walked with the same gangly stride. A memory stirred in Antonia's head but refused to surface. Emily was cradling her swimming bag in her arms as if it was something precious. Antonia was secretly glad Dad hadn't found a parking space outside the pool or she would have had to walk in with her.

"Here's my mobile. Ring me on the landline if you finish early," said Dad. Antonia nodded.

"See you in a couple of hours then." Dad left Antonia at the swimming-pool entrance and ran back to the car.

Antonia changed quickly and was putting her swimming bag in a locker when someone tapped her on the shoulder. She swung round and saw Emily, her curly hair escaping from her swimming hat and a silly grin on her face.

"This is for you," she said, thrusting a gift box at Antonia. "It's to say thank you, for helping me to find Stripes and for not telling on me."

"Oh!" Antonia exclaimed. "You didn't need to get me anything."

"I did," Emily insisted. "I was stupid and careless and I'm really sorry."

A small crowd of Year Six girls gathered round the lockers.

"Open the box," they urged.

Reluctantly, Antonia prised off the lid.

"Don't jog her," said Emily, putting out her hands to keep everyone back. "It's fragile. Do you like it, Antonia? Mum made it especially for you. It's a 'stardish'. Get it? *Stardish*, clever, huh?"

Antonia stared at the smoky-blue glass dish nestling in tissue paper. Pushing it aside with a finger she nearly dropped the box in shock. The base of the dish was resting in the curled arms of a dead starfish.

"No!" exclaimed Antonia thrusting the box back at Emily. "I can't take this."

Chapter Seven

"Of course you can." Emily handed the box back but Antonia clenched her hands and refused to take it. "Please, Antonia. You deserve it."

"No, I don't. I didn't do anything. I don't want it," she said, stepping back and bumping into the lockers.

"It's not that expensive, honest," Emily appealed to her in front of the watching girls. "Mum makes them. She's really clever with her hands."

"It's beautiful," said a girl called Rose. "Where's your mum's shop? It's my sister's birthday soon. She'd love something like that."

While Emily gave Rose directions, Antonia slipped unnoticed through the crowd and into the swimming pool. By the time Emily followed her, Antonia was safely in the pool, swimming lengths to warm up. Emily waved and mouthed something but Antonia pretended not to see her. Four swimming coaches taught the squad and, luckily for Antonia, she was put in a different group from

Emily. At the end of the training session, Antonia's coach let her group out of the water first. Antonia hared over to the changing room and changed without showering or drying her hair. Luck was still on her side. She saw in the spectators' gallery that Dad had come early to watch her swim, so she didn't have to hang around and risk bumping into Emily again.

"Where's the fire?" joked Dad, as Antonia hurried him to the car.

"I'm tired," said Antonia, slumping down into the passenger seat.

She was annoyed with herself. Why hadn't she been more truthful? She'd had the perfect opportunity to tell Emily what she thought of her parents' shop, but she'd chickened out and let her think she didn't deserve a gift.

I couldn't tell her with everyone listening in, Antonia reasoned in her head, but deep down she knew that it wasn't a good excuse. Emily's parents were in the wrong and by keeping quiet so was she. Antonia felt miserable, knowing she'd let everyone down, especially her dolphins. What would Spirit think of her now?

I'll tell Emily tomorrow, Antonia promised herself. *I'll get her on her own so I don't embarrass her.*

She spent ages in front of the mirror rehearsing what she would say. It wasn't easy, particularly because she'd promised Claudia she'd give Emily a chance. But surely Claudia didn't mean keeping quiet over

something as important as this? Antonia wished Claudia understood that Emily was as bad as her parents.

Antonia half-expected Emily to waylay her in the playground before school and try to give her the 'stardish' again, but there was no sign of any of Year Six.

"They're rehearsing for their leavers' play," said Cai, when Antonia asked where everyone was hiding. "They had to come to school early because it's the first time they've practised with costumes."

Feeling frustrated, Antonia kicked at a football heading towards her. The ball spun across the playground to Toby who, with a fancy bit of footwork, scored a goal.

"Way to go!" he cried, rushing across the

playground to high-five Antonia. "Want to be on our team?"

"No, thanks," said Antonia, grinning in spite of herself.

At lunchtime, Antonia was sitting on the field eating her packed lunch with Cai and Toby, when Emily broke away from a group of Year Sixes and came and sat next to them.

"Sorry about last night," she said, staring straight at Antonia as she pulled a cheese-and-pickle sandwich out of her lunchbox. "I didn't mean to embarrass you. Dad says I'm as subtle as an elephant in a tutu."

Antonia tried to swallow a mouthful of cake but it stuck in her throat and she ended up choking.

"Steady," said Cai, banging her on the

back as she coughed and spluttered. "Here, drink this."

He handed her his water bottle and Antonia drank from it gratefully.

"Better?"

"I'm sorry!" Emily face was bright red. "Now I've embarrassed you again. Look, if you change your mind about the stardish, then it's yours."

Antonia's eyes were smarting with tears from her choking fit. She pulled a tissue from the pocket of her dress and wiped them before blowing her nose. Her heart was thumping and her hands trembled slightly. Fragments of the speech she'd rehearsed for Emily reached her lips, only to fizzle out. She closed her eyes for a second, determined to tell Emily what she thought of her parents' shop but as she was about to begin, she remembered her promise to Claudia. Would it really be breaking that promise to say something to Emily? Maybe if she said something about conservation in general, Emily would take the hint?

"Do you like Sea Watch? Are you going to keep going?" asked Antonia.

"I love it – everyone's so friendly," said Emily. "I can't wait for the summer holidays when I can spend all day there."

"Have you done any conservation work before?"

"Nah." Emily bit into her sandwich. "I've not really been into stuff like that. I keep telling you, I joined to make friends."

"The work we do at Sea Watch is very important. If we don't look after the sea life then there'll be nothing left for the future," said Antonia.

"Yeah, Claudia already told me that but let's face it, there's not much we can do about it, is there? We're just kids."

"There's loads you can do," said Antonia earnestly, "You could—"

"Is that the time?" Emily wolfed down the rest of her sandwich as she checked her watch. "Sorry, but I've got to go. Rehearsals start in five minutes and I need the loo. Are you going to Sea Watch after school?"

Cai nodded.

"Great," she added. "Eleanor and Karen are coming too. We'll walk with you. Wait

94

for us by the gates." Emily scrambled to her feet, accidentally treading on Cai's lunchbox. "Whoops, sorry. Don't think I broke it. See you guys later, then."

"Well done," said Toby a huge grin stretching across his face. "Antonia scares another person off with a lecture on conservation."

"I don't lecture!" Antonia protested.

"He's only joking," said Cai laughing. "Toby's as keen on conservation as we are, he's just too busy playing football to help at Sea Watch. I mean, where would the world be without football?"

"That's right," chuckled Toby good-naturedly. "I'm preserving the game, so there's something left for the future."

"Very funny," said Antonia, forcing a laugh. But on the inside she was frustrated at her failure to talk to Emily. Then suddenly she remembered and said, "I thought we were going to the harbour after school tonight?"

"Oh, I forgot to say. Aunty Claudia doesn't think it's a good idea. She said it would be better to wait until we see the boat again."

Toby put his rubbish back in his lunchbox. "I'll leave you guys to it," he said. "I'm going to play football."

"Wait for me," said Cai. "Do you want to play, Antonia?"

"No thanks," said Antonia, sore with disappointment. She didn't want to wait until the fishing boat did more damage. She wanted to try and find it now, and she'd been looking forward to playing detective at the harbour all day. The boys sprinted off, leaving Antonia alone.

Moments later a shadow fell over her and she looked up to see Lauren and Becky's sneering faces.

"Well, look who it is. Billy-no-mates," said Lauren.

Becky chuckled.

"Shall we ask her to play with us?"

"No!" said both girls together and, giggling, they walked away.

Suddenly Antonia longed for Sophie. They'd been friends for ever. A proper chat with Sophie was just what Antonia needed to cheer her up.

Miss Brown was not in a good mood after lunch and gave 5B a written task that had to be done in silence. Antonia finished hers with time to spare and was told to read.

She didn't feel like reading. Her mind kept wandering to her disappointment about not going to the harbour after school. It was all Emily's fault. If only she'd been more careful locking Stripes's cage, then Antonia and Cai could have explored the harbour yesterday. Emily had made it awkward for Antonia at swimming club and now she was muscling in on her friendship with Cai.

Antonia was finding it hard to trust Claudia's words, when she was sure that the girl was as bad as her parents. Antonia sighed. She'd had more than enough of

Emily today. When the home-time bell finally rang, she couldn't face seeing her again, so she waylaid Cai as he left the classroom.

"I'm not coming to Sea Watch tonight."

Cai stopped in surprise. "Everything all right?" he asked.

"Yes, I've just got a bit of a headache."

Antonia couldn't look at Cai, in case he guessed she wasn't telling the truth.

"Bad luck. I expect it was all that writing. Are you sure you don't want to come to Sea Watch? You can sit up at the house until your head clears."

"Thanks, but no," said Antonia.

"Looks like it's me and Emily then." Cai pulled a face. "She's all right, but I wish she

didn't talk so much. I hope you feel better soon."

"Thanks," said Antonia.

Chapter Eight

Antonia walked home slowly, trying not to think about all the exciting things she would be missing at Sea Watch. It was very hot and Sandy Bay Road seemed steeper than usual. Antonia stopped when she reached the top and sat on the wooden bench overlooking the bay to get her breath back. The sea was

packed with swimmers. Antonia imagined floating in the cool salty water and suddenly she had a strong urge to be in the sea. She wasn't allowed to swim without an adult, but Claudia often let her and Cai paddle from her private beach.

"I should have gone to Sea Watch," Antonia told an inquisitive wren watching from a nearby bush.

She closed her eyes, savouring the warm sun on her face. Immediately her thoughts turned to Emily. Why had she let the new girl put her off from going? There was room for everyone at Sea Watch, regardless of whether you liked them or not. And why didn't she like Emily? Was it just because of her parents' shop? Antonia knew she wasn't being fair. It was wrong to blame Emily for her parents' behaviour. But that wasn't the only problem. Deep down, Antonia was a little scared that Emily might steal Cai away. The moment she admitted it, Antonia knew it was a ridiculous fear. She and Cai had an extra-special friendship cemented by their amazing secret, the Silver Dolphins. Cross with herself, Antonia jumped up, startling the wren into flying away chattering loudly.

"I've been such an idiot!" she exclaimed.

She decided to turn back and go to Sea Watch, but then a strong sense that Spirit needed urgent help came over her. The feeling was too intense to ignore. School bag bumping against her back, Antonia sprinted for Gull Bay, knowing her favourite beach

would be quieter than Sandy Bay. She was halfway down the lane when her dolphin charm began to vibrate. Its silver tail thrashed against her neck, urging her into the sea. Antonia touched the charm with her left hand, pleased that once again she'd sensed Spirit's call before it had happened.

"Spirit, I hear you," she whistled as the silver dolphin charm broke into a piercing whistle.

On the sand, Antonia stopped to pull off her socks and sandals. There were a handful of people in the cove, dedicated sun worshippers plugged into their iPods or reading books while their bodies tanned. Unnoticed, Antonia left her sandals and bag high up the beach then ran down to the water.

Silver Dolphin, called her necklace, its soft body thrashing against her neck.

"I'm coming," Antonia clicked back.

She splashed into the water, shivering at the icy coldness of it on her hot feet. As soon as the sea reached her waist, Antonia lunged forward, her legs melding together like a tail as she swam. Becoming a Silver Dolphin was something she could never tire of. Antonia arched her body, leaping in and out of the water as she raced to answer Spirit's call. She swam for ages until Gull Bay was a tiny dot in the distance, but still the only sign of Spirit was his frantic whistling. Antonia concentrated on swimming like a dolphin and to her delight, she swam faster than ever before. Then suddenly she felt vibrations in the water, tapping like raindrops against her skin. Altering her course slightly, Antonia swam in the direction of the vibrations. They were rapidly growing much stronger and made her uneasy. Something must be very wrong to disturb the sea in such a violent manner.

"Spirit, where are you?" she whistled.

"Not far," Spirit clicked. "I can feel you approaching."

A short while later, Antonia sensed the source of the vibrations was deeper underwater and dived down. She passed a dolphin, then another, then a large group who parted for her.

"Silver Dolphin," they clicked, nodding in relief as she swam between them. Up ahead the water was swirling manically. Antonia swam on, passing Bubbles, Dream and their mother, Star, then a small group of dolphins who were keeping another dolphin back, gently butting her with their noses each time she tried to swim past.

"My baby!" cried the dolphin with such anguish, Antonia went ice-cold and her swimming faltered.

"Hurry, Silver Dolphin," called Spirit and Antonia forced herself to swim on.

At last, she saw Spirit's magnificent silver body twisting in the water as he and another large dolphin struggled with something. With a final burst of energy, Antonia sped up and reached the large dolphins. She saw they were wrestling with a net.

"Topper's stuck," said Spirit, tugging on a frayed piece of rope.

For a second, Antonia's brain froze and it felt as if she was watching the scene from far away. Topper, a baby dolphin, flailed around, screaming in panic as the net bit into his soft skin. His mother screamed back, her high-pitched whistle so piercing, Antonia found it impossible to think. Then suddenly another voice sounded in her head.

Claudia.

Her voice, low and soothing, helped Antonia to blot out the panicked sounds around her.

Stay calm, Silver Dolphin. You can do this.

At once, Antonia's brain began working again. How long had Topper been trapped?

Dolphins could stay underwater for an hour but they usually surfaced every ten minutes for air. The biggest danger to Topper right now was that he might suffocate and drown. Immediately Antonia knew what she must do. She swam to Spirit and tapped him lightly on the side to get his attention.

Chapter Nine

pirit didn't look round. "Help us, Silver Dolphin," he said, still tugging on the net.

Antonia pointed upwards. "Let's take him to the surface where he can breathe," she said. "Then we can concentrate on freeing him."

"Good idea." Spirit butted the other dolphin, still frantically pulling at the net.

"Cracker, help us get your son to the surface."

The other dolphin was so intent on freeing his baby, he didn't respond until Antonia caught hold of his fin.

"Topper needs air," she said firmly. "Help us."

It was hard and dangerous work trying to get Topper to the surface. The baby dolphin was thrashing so violently, Antonia was scared that Spirit, Cracker, or even she might get caught up in the net. She was also worried about the harm the dolphin would inflict on himself. She'd seen small beads of blood in the water coming from a cut on Topper's tail.

"Topper," she clicked. "Listen to me. You're safe now. We're going to help you, but you

must stop wriggling. Lie still."

Topper was too scared to listen to Antonia's soothing clicks and continued to throw himself about. The net and the dolphin were heavy and Antonia wished she was stronger, when suddenly she realised more help had arrived.

"Cai!" she gasped. "Thank goodness."

Cai caught hold of a piece of the net, adding his force with everyone else as they pulled upwards. Gradually, Topper began to calm down. Glancing across, Antonia realised it wasn't a good sign. The baby dolphin's eyes were glazed and his nose had turned a strange colour.

"Hurry," clicked Antonia, pulling the net with a strength she never realised she had.

At last they surfaced. Topper lay very still.

"Hold the net tight, don't let it sink," said Antonia as she edged her way closer to him.

Moving across the wet rope was harder than it looked. It was slippery and Antonia's feet caught in the squares. Cai, Spirit and Cracker stretched the net as taut as they could, while Antonia clambered towards Topper. She moved quickly but carefully, knowing that Topper's life depended on her, and finally, she reached the dolphin. He was still breathing, but only just. Antonia clasped his tiny head in her hands and very gently breathed into his partly opened mouth. Topper didn't stir. Antonia continued to help the dolphin to breathe until Topper made a funny choking sound, then gulped at the air.

"Steady," soothed Antonia, stroking the side of his face. Topper's eyes rolled and Antonia felt his body stiffen as he focused on her.

"You're safe now," she whispered. "The Silver Dolphins are here to help you."

Antonia began to work the net away from Topper's body. It was a slow process. The wet rope bit into her fingers and she had to be careful not to damage Topper's soft skin as she worked to free him.

"I need something sharp," she said, vowing to carry a small pair of scissors around with her, in future.

"A rock would do," called Cai. "If Spirit and Cracker can manage here, I'll go look for one."

"Arrow can take your place," clicked Spirit.

Antonia looked up and saw that they were surrounded by anxious-looking dolphins. Spirit's pod must have followed them to the surface. Arrow, a muscular animal with a bold yellow stripe, swam forward and took Cai's place. Antonia continued to work on the ropes, even as the saltwater made her sore fingers sting. She'd half-freed Topper when she noticed a red stain leaching towards her. Casually, Antonia moved along to examine Topper's tail. It was worse than she'd thought. A nasty cut stretched the length of Topper's tail fin so that it dangled like a broken limb. He also had rope burn and ugly wealds stretching across his silver skin.

Antonia looked to the bleeding first, laying her hands on Topper's tail, willing the cut to

heal. *Mend*, she thought and in her mind, imagined the damaged skin coming together to stop the bleeding. The picture in her head became more and more vivid and a warm feeling spread down Antonia's hands. Her fingers began to prickle. The sensation wasn't as painful as it had been the first time she'd done this – the first time she used her Silver Dolphin powers to heal. She must be getting better at it!

Antonia continued to press firmly down on Topper's tail until the prickling sensation in her fingers calmed and the warm glow spread again through her hands. She held them against Topper for a minute longer, then slowly pulled them away. The tail had healed cleanly, leaving only a faint puckered line of skin. Antonia healed the rope burns next. When she'd finished, she was exhausted and her hands were as limp as seaweed. Topper stared at Antonia in awe, then weakly flapped his tail.

Cai had returned and was watching Antonia while clutching two small rocks.

"Wow!" he clicked. "That was fantastic. How long did it take you to learn to do that? Will you teach me?" He faltered, as Antonia shook her long blond hair over her face.

"Oh, you can't, can you?" Cai said wistfully. "It's one of your extra powers, isn't it?"

Antonia nodded, wishing that Cai didn't look so disappointed. Claudia and Spirit had warned her that being a very powerful Silver Dolphin was a big responsibility. She thought

she had understood, but now she was beginning to realise how it would affect her in others ways, too.

"Clever you, finding two rocks," she said, quickly changing the subject.

Cai handed the rocks to Antonia but she refused to take them.

"You free Topper," she said. "You found the rocks, so it's only fair."

Cai smiled gratefully and set to work sawing at the rope with the rocks. Gradually the netting fell away and Antonia rolled it up to prevent any further accidents. Cracker hovered close by and when Topper was free, he swam to his son and nuzzled him on the head. Then Topper's mum, a pretty young dolphin called Grace, was allowed near the disintegrating net. There was a joyful reunion of nose rubbing and stroking with flippers. Grace kept thanking the Silver Dolphins, until Spirit kindly shooed her away with her son.

"Topper needs to rest," he said. "And the Silver Dolphins must get this rope ashore before it injures more creatures."

"Can we help, Dad?" asked Bubbles, who was hovering nearby with Dream and Star.

"I'm not sure that's a good idea," said Star, but Spirit waved her concerns away. "It'll be perfectly safe if the net is kept in a bundle. The Silver Dolphins have a long swim back to shore. They could do with some help."

Cai trod water in a slow circle. "Where is the shore?" he asked. "I don't remember how I got here. The sea all looks the same – blue!"

"That's something I can teach you," said Dream, swimming forward. "Make a clicking sound like this." She demonstrated. "Then listen for an echo. When the clicking sound hits land, it bounces back. With practice, you can work out how far away the shore is, as well its direction."

"Cool," said Cai, experimenting a few times. "I think I've got the hang of it."

Antonia and Cai folded the net into an even tighter bundle, then secured it with a loose end. Then they began towing it ashore with Bubbles and Dream.

"Where are we going?" asked Bubbles.

"Aunty Claudia's beach," and "Gull Bay," said Cai and Antonia together.

They laughed.

"I left my things on Gull Bay beach," said Antonia, "but it would make more sense to go back to yours and use the Sea Watch bins to get rid of the net. I can get my things later."

"Where did the net come from?" mused Cai. "Was it dumped on purpose?"

Bubbles stopped swimming and excitedly smacked his tail on the water.

"Dad meant to tell you, but in the drama, I expect he forgot. Some of the dolphins saw that fishing boat again, the one that's been causing the damage. There was an old net, like this one hanging from the boat rail."

"Why didn't someone call us when the dolphins first saw the boat?" asked Antonia.

"It was going too fast. It was gone before the dolphins found Dad."

Antonia's grey-green eyes blazed with fury. "This has to stop," she said in a low voice. "Topper could have died. We must find out who owns that boat and deal with them before it's too late."

Chapter Ten

Bubbles and Dream left the Silver Dolphins in sight of Claudia's beach. They rubbed goodbye with their noses and Bubbles did the twister, leaping up and standing on the surface of the sea on his tail, while he turned a full circle.

"Show off," teased Dream, before launching

into a series of arches, her silver body flashing in and out of the water.

Cai and Antonia swam the final distance home, struggling under the weight of the net, now there were only two of them to tow it. As they waded ashore, Antonia wished that after binning the net she could go back to the sea to practise arching and leaping like Bubbles and Dream. She knew it was impossible, though. Now she wasn't needed the magic was fizzling out. Her legs were working properly and water poured from her clothes as she headed up the beach. The net felt even heavier on land. Limp bits of seaweed snagged in its frayed squares, as Cai and Antonia rolled and dragged it along. When Cai stopped at the Sea Watch boat to retrieve his shoes, Antonia started to giggle.

"I've just had a thought. I haven't got any shoes to walk back to Gull Bay," she chuckled.

Cai laughed too, so much so that they both ended up rolling around in hysterics on the sand, until Claudia came from the garden to see what the noise was about.

"I'll drive Antonia home," she offered. "We'll stop off on the way to pick up your shoes and bag."

Antonia had to wait until all the jobs were finished before Claudia could take her home. She borrowed some socks from Cai and an ancient pair of welly boots from Claudia, so she could help finish the day's tasks. One by one, the volunteers drifted home until only

Emily was left. She came out of the back room from cleaning out the guillemots, carrying a sack of rubbish.

"I didn't know you were here. Why are you wearing those?" she asked, staring at Antonia's feet.

"I got my shoes wet," Antonia fibbed.

"How did you do that?"

"Um... taking some samples of the sea water."

"Oh, right. And where did you disappear to?" Emily rounded on Cai. "Skiving, I bet."

Antonia was starting to get irritated with Emily's questions. Reminding herself that Emily was only trying to be friendly, she forced a smile and said, "Did you remember to bring your camera, Emily? Some of the guillemots are almost ready to be released."

"I forgot again!" squeaked Emily, stamping her foot and narrowly missing treading on Cai. "And Mum's really keen to see some pictures. She's wondering if she could use guillemot feathers for some of her souvenirs."

"Dropped ones only, I hope," called Claudia lightly.

"Er, yeah, I suppose so," said Emily. "I don't get involved that much in the shop." She lowered her voice and said confidingly, "To be honest, it's really boring. Mum and Dad said I could work in the shop over the summer holidays, but I'd much rather be here with you lot."

"That's nice," Claudia smiled warmly at Emily. "And if your mum and dad have a spare

moment, they're welcome to come along with you to see what we do. They might find it useful. Conservation is very good for tourism. It's important to look after the environment. If we ruin the sea, then people won't want to visit and spend money in the local shops."

"Thanks," said Emily beaming back at Claudia. "I'll tell them that."

"I'm going outside to check on Stripes, so I'll put the rubbish out for you. Thanks for all your help, Emily. Will we see you tomorrow?"

"Nah. It's the play tomorrow," said Emily. "Wish me luck. I dunno why they gave me a speaking part, when I've only been here a few days. I hope I don't muck it up."

She accidentally knocked the rubbish sack against Claudia's leg as she handed it over, then waving cheerfully, went home. Antonia smothered a sigh of relief. It was hard work being nice to Emily. But clever Claudia! She hoped Emily would remember to tell her parents about the invitation.

"That's it, then," said Claudia. "We're almost done."

"Can I come with you to check on Stripes?" asked Antonia.

"Yes, of course."

Stripes was fast asleep. Claudia checked the padlock on her pen, then went back to the Sea Watch building to double check she'd locked that too, before heading up to the house for her car keys. Antonia clumped up the drive with Cai to help open the gates.

On the way to Gull Bay, Cai sat in the front

of the car and told Claudia about rescuing Topper.

"It was clever of you to get him above the water," said Claudia, glancing at Antonia in the rear-view mirror.

"I couldn't have done it without Cai," said Antonia modestly. "It was his idea to cut Topper free with the rocks." Her fingers strayed to her silver dolphin charm and she lightly stroked it, loving the way it felt just like a real dolphin.

"I'm so glad there are two Silver Dolphins," said Claudia. "You're stronger as a team."

Claudia stopped the car at the top of the track that led to the cove and Antonia and Cai walked down to the beach to get Antonia's things. Back in the car, Antonia changed out of the borrowed wellies and into her sandals.

"Thanks," she said as Claudia pulled up outside her house. "See you tomorrow."

Jessica must have been watching for her from the window because she pounced on Antonia as soon as she got in.

"Come and see my new camp in the garden," she begged. "I spent ages making it. Mum says we can eat in it, if we want to."

"Antonia, is that you?" Mum called out from the kitchen. "Good. You're just in time for tea. Do you want it in the garden with Jessica?"

"Yes, she does," called Jessica.

"Jess!" Antonia laughed. "Oh all right. I'll eat in your camp. Stop pulling on my arm."

"Hello, stranger," said Mum as Antonia

walked into the kitchen. "Did you have a good time?"

"Amazing," said Antonia, giving Mum a hug. "Can I do anything?"

"Make some drinks for you and Jessica, then take them outside with this dish of salad. I'll bring the pizza and jacket potatoes out in a minute."

Antonia loaded a tray with two glasses of peach juice and a salad bowl piled high with carrot sticks, cucumber, cherry tomatoes and red pepper. She tore off two pieces of kitchen roll for wiping fingers on and carried the tray out to the garden. Jessica had built her camp in the same place as before, only this time she'd used a huge tarpaulin sheet borrowed from Dad.

"This is wicked," said Antonia, setting the tray down and crawling inside. "Did you build it yourself?"

"Mum helped," said Jessica. "That sheet thing was too heavy for me to lift on my own. It's much better than the blanket tent because it's bigger. I'm going to ask Mum if I can sleep in it tonight. Do you want to sleep out with me?"

"Sounds fun," said Antonia. "But Mum won't let you on a school night. Why don't you ask if you can sleep out at the weekend?"

"Yes!" exclaimed Jessica, her eyes shining. "She'll have to let me — cos it's my birthday on Sunday! It could be my birthday treat."

"You're already having a birthday treat," said Antonia. "Dad's taking you to the water

park with Naomi on Saturday."

"So?" said Jessica, dismissively. "I want to sleep in the garden too." She picked up a slice of cucumber and began to nibble the rind. "Is this all we're having for tea?"

"There's pizza and jacket potatoes. I'll go and get it."

Antonia crawled out of the tent and stood up. She was facing the bay and as she turned to go back indoors, something caught her eye. She stared more carefully at the sea. In the distance, she could just make out a small blue boat. Her heart began to thump and her head felt dizzy. Was this the boat that had caused so much trouble? Antonia stood and stared but as the boat drew nearer, she groaned. It wasn't the boat she was looking for; it had a

sail and a mast. Disappointed, she went indoors to get the pizza.

Chapter Eleven

he following day, there was chaos at school as Year Six prepared for their production. There were two shows, an afternoon matinee and an evening performance. The excitement was infectious and after lunch, the Year Five teachers abandoned lessons and held a friendly rounders match instead. Not that it was ever going to be friendly with Mr Jeffers' class. They were so competitive. Right from the start, 5J were out to win, but 5B weren't going to let it happen without a fight. Even Lauren managed to put aside her dislike of Antonia, throwing her a ball so she could stump out 5J's Millie Jackson. It was a closely fought match, but in the end 5J won by one rounder.

"Cheats!" bellowed Lauren as they made their way in from the field.

"Lauren!" Miss Brown frowned at the big girl. "Any more of that and you won't play next time."

Antonia had been looking forward to going to Sea Watch all day, but once she was finally there, she couldn't settle. She kept wondering

where the old blue fishing boat was and whether it was causing any more damage. The incident with Topper had been too close for comfort. Antonia shuddered at what might have happened had she and Cai been unable to reach the baby dolphin in time.

Claudia let Antonia feed Stripes again. It was sad knowing that this was probably the last time she would see the cub.

"I hope you make friends with the other badgers. And just you be careful crossing roads when you're finally released," Antonia told Stripes.

She washed and sterilised Stripes's bottle then went to help Cai with the last few tidying jobs of the day.

Antonia ran most of the way home, but she

still couldn't get rid of her restlessness. Jessica was the same, but for a different reason. She was so excited about her birthday treat the following day that at bedtime she couldn't sleep and begged her big sister to read her a story. Antonia collected together a heap of books, including one about a family of mice living in a rusty car. She was three chapters into the mouse story when Jessica grunted and Antonia realised her sister was fast asleep.

She tiptoed out of the room and climbed the stairs to her attic bedroom. For a while she stared out of the window at the bay. The Sandy Bay Rowing Club were out in their bright green canoes, hurtling from one side of the bay to the other. At last Antonia went and

had a shower, then pulling her blind to darken the summer evening, she climbed into bed.

She slept lightly and woke very early Saturday morning, with a funny feeling that something was about to happen. Knowing she couldn't get back to sleep, she got up and pulled on some clothes. The feeling was growing stronger and was very unsettling.

Pulling open her blind, Antonia froze. A blue fishing boat was anchored near the headland cliffs. Her heart lurched sideways and she clutched at her chest with her hand. She knew this was the boat she'd been looking for. She could feel it. Hurriedly she crept downstairs to get dad's binoculars from the utility room.

Antonia took the binoculars into the

garden. The lawn was wet with dew, soaking her sandals as she crossed it. With shaking hands, she held the binoculars to her eyes, focusing them quickly, then scanning the sea until she found the boat. It *was* the right one – and it also had a tiny speedboat attached to one side. On deck, a man and a woman dressed in wetsuits were hauling a net aboard. Antonia trained the binoculars on them. It was definitely the same lady that she'd seen before, and there was something about her that was very familiar. Antonia continued to watch her. With that funny loping gait she looked and moved just like Emily. And hadn't Emily said that her parents loved scuba diving? Suddenly, there was no doubt left in Antonia's mind. These people

were Mr and Mrs Jones! She watched as the net slid on to the boat. It was full of sea life. So, she'd been right. They were stealing from the ocean!

Quickly, Antonia trained the binoculars on the boat's stern and read the boat's name and registration number aloud, "*Georgie Girl*, SB 890."

"Got you!" she cried, racing back indoors to write the details down. But as she scribbled them on the kitchen notepad a thought struck her. What exactly were Emily's parents diving for this time? They weren't far from the pink sea fan coral beds. What if they went back to collect the fragile corals? Antonia couldn't let that happen. She tapped the pencil on the pad. She knew she ought to ring the coastguard station and let the coastguard deal with it, but she didn't know the telephone number. She could go there and tell him in person, but it was a twenty-minute walk away and she felt certain there wasn't time. That left only one option. To stop Mr and Mrs Jones herself.

Antonia knew that as a special Silver Dolphin she could use her magical powers at any time, if the need arose. Surely there was a need now, before more damage was done to the coral beds? Flicking the notepad over a page, Antonia wrote a message to her parents, saying that she'd gone for an early morning walk. Then she quietly let herself out of the back door and headed for Sandy Bay.

Chapter Twelve

The air felt fresh and clean as Antonia ran along the deserted roads. She reached Sandy Bay beach in record time and, pulling her sandals off, jogged across the empty sand. It was a wonderful feeling, being alone on the beach. Antonia dumped her sandals on the rocks then hopped down to the sea. Tiny waves lapped the shore, licking at her feet as she splashed into the water.

"I am a Silver Dolphin," she whispered as the water curled over her knees. The sea was so cold it almost took her breath away. When it was waist high, Antonia gritted her teeth and swam. At first nothing seemed to be happening. Her T-shirt and shorts dragged in the water as she struggled on.

"I am a Silver Dolphin," she repeated, ignoring the sea's numbing coldness.

Suddenly a warm feeling tingled through her. At last, the magic was working! Antonia whooped in delight as her legs melded together and her body became streamlined. Seconds later she leapt from the water, whistling like a real dolphin as her body arched above the flat sea.

At first, Antonia concentrated on swimming. Her tail-like legs propelled her forward and her hands flicked at the water like fins. Soon she was swimming as fast as she had on the day she'd rescued Topper; even faster than a real dolphin. As Antonia neared the *Georgie Girl* she could see it was deserted. Mr and Mrs Jones must be off looking for more treasures in the speedboat. She was about to alter her course to go after them when she realised she needed a plan.

She couldn't confront Mr and Mrs Jones in the middle of the sea. Antonia knew she risked them discovering the secret of the Silver Dolphins if they saw her swimming alone and without diving equipment. But she had to do something to stop them or they would cause terrible damage, especially if they were plundering the coral beds. Antonia continued to swim towards the *Georgie Girl* while she thought about her dilemma. The answer came to her suddenly.

Spirit.

Most people loved watching dolphins. If Mr and Mrs Jones saw Spirit, they'd be so excited they'd probably follow him. Spirit could lead them away from the coral beds while Antonia swam back to tell the coastguard. Excited with this simple solution, Antonia stopped swimming and trod water.

"Spirit," she whistled. "I need your help."

There was a gentle swell in the sea. Muscles tensed, Antonia bobbed up and

down with the waves as she listened for a reply. It came more quickly than she'd hoped.

"Silver Dolphin, is that you?"

"Yes. Come now. I need your help."

"I'm coming, Silver Dolphin."

The sea sparkled like sapphires as the sun rose higher, but Antonia hardly noticed. She was too anxious to relax. Soon she felt the vibrations. Something was heading towards the *Georgie Girl*, travelling fast and close to the sea's surface. But the vibrations were too big to be Spirit, so Antonia dived under the water to hide. A speedboat roared up, slowing as it approached the *Georgie Girl* until the noise of the engine turned to idle. Antonia heard voices, but they were muffled, like the underwater sounds at a swimming pool.

Cautiously she swam closer, staying on the opposite side of the *Georgie Girl* to the speedboat. The closer Antonia got to the boat, the stronger her sense of unease grew. Bad things were happening and it made the hairs on the back of her neck stand up like miniature soldiers. Shivering, Antonia decided to wait where she was for Spirit. Thankfully he came quickly and, feeling his vibrations in the water, Antonia clicked his name.

"Spirit?"

"Nearly there, Silver Dolphin."

"Take care, the boat owners have returned."

"I can see them," Spirit clicked. "They're loading dive bags on to the bigger boat."

A heavy feeling lodged in Antonia's stomach. They were too late! Mr and Mrs Jones had already completed their raid. When Spirit reached her and greeted her by rubbing noses, Antonia sadly rubbed back.

"Well done, Silver Dolphin," Spirit clicked. "You did well to call me."

"But we're too late," said Antonia.

Just then the speedboat engine roared to life. Antonia and Spirit froze, but the boat raced off in the opposite direction.

"They're going back for more!"

Antonia was outraged. "Can you swim and distract them? I'll go and find out what they've been collecting, then I'll swim back to shore and tell the coastguard."

"Careful, Silver Dolphin," warned Spirit.

"Remember, we work in secret. Don't get caught."

"I won't," said Antonia. "And you take care too. Mr and Mrs Jones might net you next."

Spirit clicked a laugh. "They would have a hard job."

He started to swim away, then quickly circled back. "I'll call for the other Silver Dolphin too. You might need help."

Spirit opened his mouth and began to whistle. A shiver of excitement tingled down Antonia's spine. Her fingers strayed to her own silver dolphin charm and she clasped hold of it. The charm felt alive, its tiny body throbbing in her hand. Inside her head, Antonia heard a faint sound. Was it Cai answering Spirit's call? She closed her eyes and listened, but the noise slipped away like soft sand in an hourglass. Spirit nudged her gently in the side. Antonia's eyes flew open in surprise. For a moment, she'd forgotten where she was.

"The Silver Dolphin is on his way. Wait for him. I'm going after the boat," said Spirit.

Antonia didn't want to wait. She wanted to go aboard the *Georgie Girl* and see what Emily's parents had been collecting, but she didn't dare argue with Spirit. Impatiently, she trod water while she waited for Cai.

Chapter Thirteen

Cai arrived faster than Antonia thought he would and wasn't even out of breath. His face fell when he saw Antonia, but he recovered quickly, exclaiming, "You beat me! I was sure I'd be first this time. Where's Spirit?"

Quickly, Antonia explained everything and

when she'd finished Cai said, "So you were right about Emily's parents. I'm sorry I laughed at you."

"It doesn't matter."

It wasn't Cai's fault that he didn't have Antonia's sixth sense, but she was glad that he knew now that she hadn't imagined it all.

Quickly they swam to the *Georgie Girl* and climbed up the ladder. Antonia went first and when she reached the top she gasped in disbelief at the horror on board. The deck was covered with shallow trays, each filled to the brim with sea creatures. Writhing starfish, baby crabs frantically waving little claws, sea horses, sea urchins, there were even a few small fish with their mouths open, gasping for breath as they fried in the early morning sun.

"Quick. Help me get them back to the sea before they die," cried Antonia.

She picked up the tray nearest to her and staggering under the weight of it, tipped it over the side of the boat. Animals spun through the air, tangled together like jewellery, then slowly sunk in the bright blue water. Antonia picked up a second tray and Cai grabbed one too.

"I never thought Emily's parents would be bad enough to kill animals. It's so cruel leaving them in the sun to dry out," cried Cai.

"I knew they were bad," muttered Antonia, emptying the tray overboard and going back for another. "These are stolen treasures. The animals belong to the sea."

She stooped for another tray, then jumped

back as a small fish flipped itself on to the deck. Both she and Cai tried to pick it up, but it was thrashing wildly and was too slippery. Then suddenly, the fish stopped moving and its eyes clouded over. Swiftly, Antonia lifted it with cupped hands.

"Heal," she whispered. "Please heal."

A warm sensation shot down her arms and into her fingers. Antonia prepared herself for the prickling to start. But the warm feeling was disappearing. It was as if the magic had suddenly stopped working.

Heal. Antonia willed the fish to live, but its eyes were unfocused, its mouth wide open.

Antonia swallowed, knowing it was too late. The magic wasn't working because the fish was dead. She felt a hand on her arm.

Cai gave her a comforting squeeze then ran his hand through his springy dark hair.

"Bad luck," he said. "But there are others left to save."

Antonia snapped out of her trance. Cai was right. There were still more creatures to help and they couldn't hang around. Hurriedly, she helped Cai return the remaining animals to the sea. As the last tray of creatures slid overboard, Antonia sensed danger.

"Quickly," she said, pulling Cai to the ladder of the *Georgie Girl*. "We've got to go."

Antonia went first, diving from the ladder into the sea. Cai followed and together they swam away from the boat. Feeling lots of vibrations in the water, Antonia slowed to

listen. The shorter ones were coming from Spirit.

"Silver Dolphins, get away from the boat," he clicked. "It's not safe."

The longer vibrations soon turned into the distinct hum of the speedboat. Antonia wished she could turn back to see the look on Mr and Mrs Jones's faces when they discovered their catch had mysteriously disappeared. She could tell from Cai's grin that he was obviously thinking the same thing. They swam underwater to meet Spirit and found him sheltering round the other side of the headland. To Antonia and Cai's delight, Bubbles, Dream, Star, Cracker and Arrow were with him.

"Well done, Silver Dolphins," Spirit clicked.

"Between us we have temporarily saved the coral beds. When those people saw me, they stopped collecting the pink sea fans and I was able to lead them back to their speedboat. I called for more dolphin help and we put on a show to give you time to search the bigger boat. When we finally gave the people the slip, I left some of the dolphins to watch the coral beds and alert me if they return."

"We'll go to see the coastguard now. He'll make sure they don't come back,' said Antonia grimly. "It was horrible on board the *Georgie Girl*. There were hundreds of animals all dying in the sun."

Bubbles swam alongside Antonia and nuzzled her with his nose. Gratefully, Antonia rubbed him back.

"Come back to mine and we'll ask Aunty Claudia to ring the coastguard," said Cai.

"That's a good idea," said Antonia. "They're friends, aren't they? He'll listen to Claudia and act straightaway."

Hurriedly, Antonia and Cai said goodbye to the dolphins. Antonia saved her goodbye to Bubbles until last.

"Seaweed tag next time, Silver Dolphin," he whispered.

"Definitely," said Antonia, managing a smile.

Cai had swum out from Claudia's beach, so they arranged to meet back at Sea Watch after Antonia had collected her shoes from Sandy Bay.

"Can you ask Claudia to ring my parents?"

said Antonia. "I left a note saying I'd gone for a walk, but that was ages ago and they might be worried."

Swimming to Sandy Bay beach, Antonia's stomach began to growl and she realised she was starving hungry. Water poured from her like rain from a drainpipe as she waded ashore and then sat on the rocks to put on her sandals. The sun was climbing in the sky and there were two other people on the beach; a man with a metal detector and a tall skinny girl collecting shells in a large bucket. As Antonia jogged across the sand, the girl stood up and waved. With a start, Antonia realised it was Emily. A low whooshing noise rushed through her head. She felt dizzy and full of white-hot anger.

Antonia marched across to the smiling Emily, intent on telling her exactly what she thought of her parents.

Chapter Fourteen

"Hello," called Emily, tripping and spilling her shells.

"Oh bother, I've been ages collecting those." She dropped on to her hands and knees to pick them up.

Antonia faltered. It was difficult to say what she wanted when she didn't have Emily's full attention.

"You're up early," she commented, wishing Emily would hurry up.

"Yeah. Mum and Dad went out on the boat, scuba diving. I can't wait to learn. Then I can go and have fun with them."

"Fun!" exclaimed Antonia. She pushed her damp hair out of her eyes and glared at the top of Emily's bent head. "Do you know exactly what your parents were scuba diving for?"

Emily stood up and stared at Antonia in surprise.

"Are you all right? You sound angry."

"I am because…" Antonia stopped, just in time. She had to be careful what she said and not give too much away about Silver Dolphins. "I heard a rumour that your parents were taking live animals from the sea, then killing them to sell in their shop."

Emily flushed bright red and her glasses slid down her nose. She pushed them back.

"I don't listen to rumours. I don't know where Mum and Dad's stock comes from, either. But I've been thinking about Sea Watch and all the good stuff that happens there. I couldn't get what Claudia said about ruining the sea and people not coming to visit any more out of my head."

Emily paused, her eyes scanning the horizon. "I like it here. I'm not sure, but I think I saw a dolphin this morning. It was quite a long way out, but it was so exciting. I'm going to come down early again tomorrow and bring binoculars.

"Anyway, I thought it would be good if

Emily's Treasure Chest concentrated on environmentally-friendly souvenirs. So I've been collecting stuff to show Mum and Dad. Dropped feathers, empty shells and even bits of driftwood."

Emily thrust the bucket at Antonia. "Look, what do you think?"

Unconsciously, Antonia touched her silver dolphin charm. It felt soft and alive. The anger slowly drained away. Claudia had been right to give Emily a chance. It wasn't fair to blame her for her parents' crimes.

"It's a brilliant idea," said Antonia. "We'll help you, Cai and me. We're often on the beach, so if we find anything pretty we'll keep it for you."

"Thanks. Well, I'd better get going. Mum

and Dad said they'd cook me breakfast when they get back. Bacon rolls with fried eggs and mushrooms. See you Monday."

Antonia lay on her back, staring up at the cloudless sky, enjoying the swell of the sea beneath her. Inside, she was still bubbling with excitement. Monday was her least favourite day of the week, but this one had been totally brilliant. It had started when Emily waylaid her and Cai in the playground before school.

"Promise you won't tell anyone," Emily whispered, pulling them into a tight huddle.

"Mum and Dad had a visit from the coastguard on Saturday. It was soooo embarrassing. Those rumours were right,

Antonia. They'd been catching sea life and letting it die, to make their souvenirs. And they'd damaged a coral bed in a special protected area! They were given a warning, but if it happens again the coastguard said he'd tell the police and they'd be prosecuted.

"Mum and Dad were really shocked. I think they knew they'd been doing wrong, but they didn't realise it was that serious. Neither of them meant to hurt anything. Mum said she didn't know that starfish and sea urchins could suffer like other animals. How dumb is that!

"They're coming with me to Sea Watch this afternoon to meet Claudia. Dad's bringing his cheque book. He's going to make a donation to Sea Watch, by way of an apology."

At the end of school, Mr and Mrs Jones met Emily and they all walked to Sea Watch with Antonia and Cai. Antonia felt uncomfortable at first, but Mr and Mrs Jones weren't the villains she'd expected them to be. They seemed genuinely upset about damaging the coral beds and the suffering they'd caused to the sea life.

They stayed at Sea Watch for ages and asked lots of questions. They were really impressed with Claudia and the work she was doing, and before they went home they made a large donation. The money meant Claudia could invest in new equipment she needed, including another pen in the garden with a pool for injured animals.

"Let's have a party," said Claudia when the

last volunteer had left.

She made a huge jug of fruit punch, peach juice and lemonade with chunks of real fruit, then put it on a tray with tall glasses, bendy straws and a dish of nibbles. They took it outside and settled themselves on the garden chairs. Antonia was on her second glass of punch when she became aware that Spirit was going to call. She put her glass on the table and seconds later, her dolphin charm began to vibrate.

"Oh!" exclaimed Cai, nearly spilling his drink. "See you later, Aunty Claudia."

Sensing the call wasn't urgent, Antonia waited for Cai and they swam to Spirit together.

Antonia was right, no one was hurt. But

Spirit had found a long piece of fishing line caught on the rocks. Cai removed it and gave it to Antonia, who tucked it in the pocket of her school dress to dispose of safely when they got home.

Spirit watched them from the sea and when they dived back into the water he said, "Thank you, Silver Dolphins. You can play with Bubbles and Dream now. You deserve a reward for all your hard work and the danger you have put yourselves in recently."

Being a Silver Dolphin was so fantastic Antonia and Cai didn't expect rewards, but it was brilliant fun playing with Bubbles and Dream. To his amazement, Cai won seaweed tag.

"My swimming's getting really good," he

boasted. "I can almost do the arms properly now."

"Flipper Boy!" teased Bubble. "But can you do a twister?"

Cai and Antonia spent ages trying. Antonia got more and more frustrated with her efforts.

"I can get three-quarters of the way round, then I collapse," she grumbled.

"You'll get there with practice," said Dream encouragingly.

"And besides, you can do everything else," said Cai.

"Not everything," said Antonia, knowing she still had lots to learn. Not just as a Silver Dolphin, but about people, too. She readily admitted her feelings about Emily had been wrong. Antonia was growing to like her and was glad she would still see Emily at Sea Watch when she left Sandy Bay Primary at the end of term.

"Flipper Feet," cried Bubbles, launching a surprise attack, butting Antonia in the back and rolling her on to her tummy. Spluttering, Antonia somersaulted and chased after him.

"Water fight," she clicked. "Two teams. You and Cai, against Dream and me."

"You're on," they all whistled back.

Bubbles leaped out of the water, turned a full circle on his tail, before landing on his side and splashing everyone.

"Oi!" laughed Cai. "Remember we're on the same team."

When everyone was thoroughly splashed Dream called a truce. "We have to go soon," she said. "Dad's taking us out to sea."

"I have to go too," said Antonia reluctantly. "Mum will worry if I'm late."

"Stay to tea," begged Cai. "We'll ring your mum when we get back. We've still got the fruit punch to finish."

"Thanks. I will if I'm allowed."

Bubbles and Dream swam with the Silver Dolphins until they were in sight of Claudia's beach.

"See you soon," clicked Antonia, rubbing noses first with Dream and then Bubbles.

She raced Cai ashore. They waded up the beach, shaking themselves like wet dogs, laughing as the water poured from their clothes. Suddenly Antonia stopped laughing and her face turned serious.